#TaraGuests

Aliena

Ukiyoto Publishing

All global publishing rights are held by

Ukiyoto Publishing

Published in 2024

Content Copyright © Aliena

ISBN 9789362698803

All rights reserved.
No part of this publication may be reproduced,
transmitted, or stored in a retrieval system, in any
form by any means, electronic, mechanical,
photocopying, recording or otherwise, without the
prior permission of the publisher.

The moral rights of the author have been asserted.

This is a work of fiction. Names, characters, businesses,
places, events, locales, and incidents are either the
products of the author's imagination or used in a
fictitious manner. Any resemblance to actual persons,
living or dead, or actual events is purely coincidental.

This book is sold subject to the condition that it shall
not by way of trade or otherwise, be lent, resold, hired
out or otherwise circulated, without the publisher's
prior consent, in any form of binding or cover other
than that in which it is published.

www.ukiyoto.com

Dedication

To the Almighty Father for the gift of ideas and awareness, and for Your immense understanding of my violent mood swings…

To my family for being there; taking care of my children when I couldn't ('cause I was so immersed in my creative pursuits) is no joke, and I'm super thankful that you continue to be there for me…

To my kids who continue to be my source of joy and headache at the same time, I'm forever amazed by your growth and development, and I'm sorry for the times I should've been there but I wasn't, for the words I said that broke your heart…

To Pat who is my first and forever supporter in all my endeavors…

To all the teachers who gave me the opportunity to discover and hone this skill, please know that despite the foul language, I'm putting your lessons to good use…

To my learners who are also headed toward this path, may you create your own and not follow the path I have trodden…

To the national leaders, abusers, enablers, and the indifferent who continue to batter Mother Earth and her children, *#TaraGuests kayong lahat*…

And to you, dear reader, may this supplement open your eyes to what's happening in the world, and may you have the strength to protect what's left of it.

ALIENA

Contents

#TaraGuests	1
Ants in a Jar	2
[Bless Me, Dear Father]	4
My Dangerous Prayer	7
#LetTheEarthBreathe	11
The Eye	13
Election	15
In the Stillness of the Night	17
Laughter	18
It's More Fun[ny] in the…	20
Enough	21
Songs of the Wee Hours	22
Songs of the Wee Hours II	24
When I Die…	26
The Wait	29
I Made a Mistake… Of Course…	31
"AI," Apo!	33
Lone Bettor	36
Coffee in Hell	38
An Ode to Our Protector	41
Equalizer?	42
Irreversible	44
Excuses	47

Lapdogs	48
that we must call our own.	48
About the Author	*49*

#TaraGuests

Tara, guests,
And have a seat at my table!
Revel in the taste of the words I serve.
Amuse, amaze, and annoy yourselves, in the echoes
Garnished with the bitterness of my homegrown herbs.
Unwind in the hot seats disarranged in a row and
Engage in a hearty conversation of the mind,
Seasoned with salt and the hottest of peppers.
Tara, guests!
Savor this moment while it lasts.

Ants in a Jar
(2023)

They sit back and watch
as on the small of our backs
we bear the load.

Standing in line
we walk back and forth,
lifting our burdens
to feed the little ones.

And as we stand and learn
to lighten our load,
our world starts to crumble
and we all scatter

without a direction,
without a goal.

All they seem to think
is that we can lift these loads forever

despite the odds.

Like ants in a jar,
our peaceful walk becomes
their eyesore,
and our chaos
gives them pleasure.

[Bless Me, Dear Father]
(2022)

Bless me, dear father,
for today, I will sin.

My ears are deaf
to the lies you spew from the pulpit,
for it is far from His mission
to fall victim to false unity.
For no one but whitewashed tombs
had conspired to have Him
impaled on a tree.

Funny how you make us weep
for the blood He shed for you and me.
It was not His purpose to fish for sympathy.
To tell you frankly, He rose in victory,
when He said, "It is done,"
and drew His final breath.

Aliena

Satan must have gone berserk,
and in desperation, did a lot of work;
for he is in a race against time
before he gets bound in the pits of hell.

So he dwells inside the clueless spirit
of the holy mortals wearing their habit,
so that he could sit them in their high horses
and cause deceit to rule the unsuspecting world.

So why would I be surprised
at your failed attempt at lies,
when your filthy hands could not even cross
the boundaries of rancid waters
just to draw sinners out?

Your tales of a 'pathetic savior'
are only cesspools of falsehoods.
Again, He did not come into this world
to cry "foul" over being tortured
to death.

So even if you stand behind your shiny, wooden pulpit,

and power our faith with your earth-shattering voice,

this, I beseech thee, dear father:

serve not thy folly upon a silver platter.

My Dangerous Prayer
(2023)

Create me in a clean heart, O God, and renew a steadfast spirit in me,

This verse had been first in my prayers since You once again called me.

You know all my sins and are faithful enough to forgive 'em,

and to cleanse me from unrighteousness, yeah that's what You said it is.

I do believe, O God, that You never really left me,

But my mind is too focused on the fire and the mud that consumed me.

I forgot who You are and Your capability to save me,

Forgot all Your promises and how most of these have helped me.

I get by everyday but am still stuck in life's routines,

Without You there's no true life, not a spirit, not a meaning.

No pain, no gain, just walls of my pride, building,

Just hate and shame and stains of my deepest sins, clinging.

You know, Lord,

I tried my best to stay away from all these sins,

But the more I distance myself the closer they come creeping in.

I'm tired of this pride,

I'm tired of the hate,

I'm tired of this pain,

I'm tired of this fear,

I'm tired of everything that keeps me from believing You're near!

Sometimes I tend to think this walk with God is worthless. Why?

One day I'm in, the next I'd go sin and then back again,

Like a light in a haunted mansion,

turning on, and off, and vice versa;

Yeah, I am lukewarm, Lord, You can just spit me out if You want to.

My light's not shining, Lord, my salt has lost its flavor,

Aliena

In fact, it's been too long since I updated my faith journal.

I don't even know if my reflections on *youversion* still make sense,

Or if I post this stuff on social media, would any of my friends believe it?

I was told to keep my words few,

Let no remain no

and yes mean yes,

But I kept on binding a word in heaven or down here in my chest.

But at the end of the day, they're all lies, all lies, all lies!

Lies that I devise just to keep my sanity intact and boost my pride.

How much more time would it take before You come back, O Jesus?

And if You ever do, would You take our hands and forgive us?

We're soaked in the mud again, but this time, in a mud of deep distress,

You know, for whatever reason, now too deep for man to comprehend.

Of all the things that happen daily in my life,

I just wanted to scream at the top of my lungs like an animal gone wild,

I'm here at the bottom, kneeling weakly on a rock,

Unaware that what holds me there was the Presence I have sought for long.

Create me in a clean heart, O God, and renew a steadfast spirit in me,

Keep Your child from sinning willfully, may they not rule over me.

Give me the grace to repent of all my sinful ways,

For all the things I've ever done that seem to spit on Your lovely face.

If You are willing, Lord, break the thick walls of my pride,

I'm tired of waking up each day just to go living in a blight.

Forgive me of my sins and help me Lord to start again,

Take my hand, O God, because without You

I'm good as dead.

#LetTheEarthBreathe
(2022)

Thick, black smoke rises into the air
from the monstrous factories,
the honking vehicles,
the burning twigs and leaves,
and the stench of cigars and vapes.

Plastics fill the once azure beach,
feeding venom to the fish,
wreaking havoc on its coral reefs.

Our soil has become barren and futile
from the downpour of chemicals
that alter God's design.

Even our weary souls
were not spared from the toxin
of fear and warmongering,
of the standards of beauty
that are beyond our reach,

of the insatiable need to stand in the spotlight,
and the undying greed for wealth and prosperity.

Our eyes, bedazzled by the wonders
of what the future offers:
the ease of work; the living dead.

It went on for many a year,
decade, and century.

But let us face the music:
Behind all these wonders
is the world that's about to breathe its last.
Diagnosed with a malignant disease
brought about by our unending voracity.

All that is left is about four-to-five years.
Time's too short to wallow in fears.
It's time to make a stand,
not by the noisy chants in the streets,
but to hold out our hands,
and save our mother earth from its nearing end.

The Eye
(2022)

No matter how heated the passion burns,
No matter how bloody the mess,
No matter how sappy the motherhood words,
No matter how massive the crowd,

Let not your heart be moved.
But keep your eyes peeled,
your forefinger on the shutter,
your pen and paper on hand,
and your story rooted from the ground.

Set your eyes on the truths
that fly from different directions.
Keep your feet swift
in gathering stories
and sending the message.

Let no one entice you to stop,
smell the roses,

and lay your weary body inside a bubble.
Let no gold or silver blind your eyes
and prompt your ink to peddle lies.

For you are not here to follow the rabid herd,
but to stand back and watch,
and by your hand, make an indelible mark
on the thick pages of our nation's book
that is yet to be completed.

Election
(2022)

Mudslinging
Gaslighting
Name-calling
Well-poisoning

These are all the norms
whenever the time comes
to choose the right hand
that will steer our nation's course.

Dirt-digging
Warmongering
Rumor-spreading
Outright lying

Will someone ever step up
and diverge from this putrid culture,
and once and for all, give us something true
to hope for and hold onto?

Our country is lagging behind,

our dream of progress remains a state of mind.

Nothing will ever propel us forward

but the courage to diverge from this long, crooked path,

and take the road less traveled by.

Unfortunately for us, no other hand will reach out and try.

It's our own tails to pull, to survive.

In the Stillness of the Night
(2022)

In the stillness of the night,
there's a candle burning bright.
in the darkness, bringing light,
peaceful, just, and fair, and right.

Laughter
(2011)

They laugh because I am the only ship amid the sea,

I laugh because their shallow bodies live on black debris;

I laugh because their eyes look down the level of their brains

when they laugh because they thought I'm just a silly, empty slate.

They laugh because I am the only rock among the sand,

I laugh because they stumble when the storm comes down to land;

I laugh because they're washed away without a single trace

when they laugh because they thought they've weathered Mother Nature's rage.

They laugh because I am the only rose among the thorns,

I laugh because they nurture sturdy, empty, stupid horns;

Aliena

I laugh because they utter every word with empty heart

when they laugh because they thought my mind was very far apart.

They laugh because I am the only spot among the clean,

I laugh because behind they dance in every shade of green;

I laugh because they savor every sheaf they didn't glean

when they laugh because they thought I had but nothing else to eat.

It's More Fun[ny] in the…
(2022)

The world trembles in fear
of great destruction at hand.

While at the far east…

people are already at war
on which *movie* is the best to watch,
and which one deserves to flop.

Enough
(2022)

of playing burned by the fire you have kindled.

Our eyes are peeled

and are on guard of your every move.

That is why every time you drown

in the cesspool of your lies,

our mouths only twitch upward,

asking ourselves,

"Are we surprised?"

Songs of the Wee Hours
(2022)

Ten in the evening.
The cicadas are singing
songs that bring me chills.

Electric fan blows
breezy wind with dancing dusts,
causing runny nose.

No more minty smell
can relieve the shooting pain
that throbs in my head.

A big, cluttered room
reeking with the smell of death:
Lizards, roaches, mice.

Through the open door,
I heard water rushing, then
the flush of a bowl.

Aliena

Loud thud on the roof
made me jolt like a rabbit.
Oh! It's just a cat.

Rooster crows aloud,
a new day is on the rise.
Three in the morning.

Songs of the Wee Hours II
(2024)

Twelve in the morning
I face my computer screen,
eyes on a new theme.

Breathing out an air
of woes, and woes, and woes of
a dark, broken world.

Chaos, left and right,
Children's unbridled unrest,
leaves our hearts shattered.

Headphones on both ears,
Listening to Oladokun,
Joy; my mind's at ease.

Through my keys, I type
sensible, nonsensical
echoes of the mind,

Aliena

Taking comfort in
Aurelius, Epictetus
Seneca, Jesus—

the only spirits
I welcome in my home in
wee hours of the nigh.

When I Die…
(2024)

When I die…

Curse me.

Swear at me.

Say all the things that you weren't bold enough
to say in my face.

Let your pent-up emotions roll out of your tongue
like the shells of a snail.

Spit at the glass of my casket,

or better yet,

throw up!

Throw up all the things you thought were good;
throw up all the lessons I taught you
with a tongue teeming with lies.

Kick the poor box down to the floor
till it breaks into pieces!
Batter my embalmed corpse
under the soles of your feet.

Beat it black.

Beat it blue.

Aliena

Beat it till the last color of life
leaves my skin without a hue.

For I could no longer get up to defend myself.
I couldn't clap back anymore
or vent about you to my co-teachers,
or report you to the Guidance Office,
or to the Principal,
or to the Police.

It wouldn't even be possible

for my ghost to haunt you in your sleep.

Let no good thing about me
come out of your mouth;
(that's plastic of you).

But go ahead and mock me
for the monster that I used to be.

Come on, don't hold back

if you don't feel like forgiving!

Let it all out.

And when time comes
when my remains parade around the city

to the sepulcher,

sing at the top of your lungs,
"Na na… na na na na… hey, hey! Goodbye!"

Take delight in the fact that I'm no longer around
to cause you hurt and pain.

Pray to God to throw my soul
to the deepest pits of hell,
where there is no peace for the wicked;
only worms, weeping, and gnashing of teeth.

Pray that you live enough to see the day I cry.
Let my endless wail be music to your ears
and a soothing balm to your broken soul.

For this is all the respect that my soul deserves,
and it would be a more vicious torture to hear

kind words,

forgiveness,

and last respects,
when you've never gotten anything from me
when I was still alive and breathing.

The Wait
(2024)

Jews wait for the "Messiah."

Christians for "Jesus."

Buddhists for "Maitreya," and

Hindus for "Krishna," or "Rama,"

or whoever it is that serves as
Vishnu's vessel.

Muslims for "Issa,"

and almost everyone for a Deus ex Machina.

They go to their congregations,
sing praises, bow in reverence;

offer their 10, 20, or hundred percent;
creating problems in their heads,
hoping for their 'savior' to come and lift them up;
judging people who are going through
the same road;

turning a blind eye to the hearts
that hunger and thirst for compassion…

If only they knew
that these 'saviors' have been there all along:

in the deepest chamber of our hearts,
waiting for us
to meet 'them' through the narrow gate.

Yet no one seems to have the courage
to take the first step.

Because most of them set their eyes
on the great, dramatic reveal.

But those saviors…
They're actually here.

I Made a Mistake... Of Course...
(2024)

I made a mistake.

Of course, people will laugh at me and forget the good things I've done.

I made a mistake.

Of course, people will have something new to 'marites' about.

I made a mistake.

Of course, people will make me feel like I'm the dumbest person in the planet.

I made a mistake.

Of course, people will make my errors viral on social media.

I made a mistake.

Of course, one of my constituents might say, "*Ano ba yan, teacher/ school paper adviser/ anyone who has **moral** ascendancy pa naman, tapos…*"

I made a mistake.

Of course, they'll mock me 'cause I'm supposed to be smarter.

I made a mistake.

Of course, one of my constituents might call me a fake news peddler by now.

I made a mistake.

Of course, I'll correct it. After all, accountability is a principle I teach to my constituents.

I made a mistake.

Of course, I'm human. I mean, is there anyone perfect in the room?

"AI," Apo!
(2024)

Passing of assignments.

*One by one, the one whole sheets of paper
dropped by the teacher's table.*

The tension in the classroom is **PALPABLE**,

as my **CONFLICTED** eyes moved from left to right,

making a **POIGNANT EXPLORATION**
of an **INTRICATE TAPESTRY** of terminologies,

that even in my ten years of service,

I wouldn't use on my four-year-old.

CERTAINLY, I couldn't **SHAKE OFF**,

this disturbing feeling
EXACERBATED by the knowledge
that many learners come to my class
without a response to the simplest questions,
but would readily give **NUANCED PERSPECTIVES**

like they've **NAVIGATED** the **REALM** of books for decades or centuries.

It had me **DELVING** into the deepest of thoughts:

What kind of thinking it **FOSTERS**,

as more and more minds cling to its incredible **INTELLIGENCE.**
It sure turns difficulty into ease,

blunt into sharp,

eyesore to a dazzle,

all in a few types and clicks.

But then, let's face it:
AS AN AI LANGUAGE MODEL,

they can only do so much

to make instant wordsmiths

out of eyes who can't even recognize a word.

But give them a pen and paper.

Ask them a question.

Give them an hour or two.

And watch as their fragile fingers tremble with the movement of their pens,

GRAPPLING for a **MULTIFACETED** response.

IN CONCLUSION, it only **UNDERSCORES** an **APPARENT** reality:
without this 'second brain,'

this generation isn't as sharp as it wants people to see.

Lone Bettor
(2024)

One, two, three million pesos.
Four, five, six billion pesos.
Six becomes seven, and ten, and then twenty,
Dropped on the same, gambling palm,
week, after week, after week, after week.

How lucky could they get.
How blessed: swimming in the lap of luxury
in a short span of time,
right before the very eyes
of the hundred and fifteen million mouths
who have the littlest idea
where to get the next meal,

or transport,

or tuition;

or even a cent for their children's provisions.

How rotten!
How vile!

Aliena

How could they watch with their dull, greedy eyes
people's blood, sweat, and sacrifice,
that were all for nothing?

Motherland is still in the quagmire of poverty,
content with relishing at the crumbs
that fall from the crocodiles' tables
when she deserves better:
the pearls, the gold, the silver,
the relief of her children who hunger,
not a series of triumphs for the same, single bettor.

One, two, three million pesos.
Four, five, six billion pesos.
Six becomes seven, and ten, and then twenty,
May all these suffice
to fill the pressing needs
of a starving country.

Coffee in Hell
(2024)

While they in the far West scream, "It's burning,"
I am inviting you to my humble territory,
where everything is "more fun" as it wants you to see.

Come, watch with me

over a steaming cup of coffee,

how our so-called 'pillars'

turn our beloved Motherland
into a realm of brimstone and ashes,

waging war with a chinky-eyed beast,

and button noses pointed up to the giants
are their only ammunition.

And alas! Multi-tasking,

Motherland's cutting its body in half,
like the infamous "Manananggal":

one country in the north,

another in the south,

like Korea in Asia,

or Carolina and Dakota in the States.

Aliena

Funny, isn't it?

While they are caught in a standoff
with the big, neighboring panda,

their eyes seemed dim
to the bigger giant inside:

the flaring fingers of Apolaki melting the earth in a swift,

scorching our skins to death,

dissolving what's left of our sanity,

drying the irrigation of wisdom and knowledge,

sucking out our vitality, our purpose, our meaning,

leaving only our bones

glued to the glitters of our laptops and phones,

our robotic limbs nurtured for an endless cycle of toil,

our stomachs twisting in hunger,

our throats drying up from thirst…

Let's watch, over a cup of coffee how our humble abode, into ashes, turns.

Breakup of the Year

(2024)

In only a matter of two years

that a sturdy Tree, bursting with Christmas colors,
pointed its tip to the dark sky,
its roots got infiltrated by red-clad termites,
and the Tree that once towered the Earth—
a sight for sore eyes—
now lays on the ground
like a long, black piece of coal.

An Ode to Our Protector
(2022)

O, Sierra Madre,
our native Great Wall,
Guardian of the East,
for centuries
You have shielded us
from the fury of the storms.

Now it's time we shelter you
from the surge of a mechanical typhoon.
If we need to scream
or take up arms against the machines,
that, will we do, just to see you
remain standing firm and tall.

Equalizer?
(2024)

Behind the screen
is a leveled playing field
where we can look straight into the eyes
them who mount on their high horses
and with our virtual tongues
drag them down the ground where we stand.

And oh, how rude,
how savage,
how heartless do we seem!
Hurling the foulest of words
like small daggers,
their downfall creating
a small, smile of triumph
in our cynical faces.

But can we stand before them,
look them in the eyes,
spit out mouthful of curses and swears,

just like we do behind the screens…

or do we just hide under the skirts
of our radioactive devices,
pretending to be fearless,
when deep inside that *mechanical* armor,
the warrior is *a child?*

Irreversible
(2024)

Six years from now, the
Earth will lie on her bed and
take her final breath.

They screamed; no answers.
They called out; we turned our backs.
They knocked; we closed doors.

"A race against time."
Bullcrap of the century.
There is no more time.

Planting trees won't help.
Eco-friendly illusions,
our futile attempt.

We only want to
stop and smell the roses and
care for nothing else.

Aliena

Smokes will keep rising,
and make thick, dark covers in
the once bright, blue sky.

They'll smother our lungs
with their foul, fluffy fingers,
'til we lose our breaths.

We will take a whiff
of the scent of coins and bills,
but won't have any.

With every leaf that
Falls, three more leaves grow out of
this tree called people.

They keep on growing
Like wildfire in a forest;
They're out of our hands.

Then we'll crawl and scratch
for a mere morsel of bread
to fill our stomachs.

And we'll hear the cry
of many hungry children
we cannot nourish.

Shall we call Jesus
to take us off this puddle
we call, "Misery"?

Maybe, maybe not.
We destroyed His Father's work.
We are not worthy.

Weep and bathe in ash,
and fast while clad in sackcloth?
It's not Bible times.

Try to turn back time?
Snap out of your delusions.
We just move forward;

onward to our end,
weeping eyes and gnashing teeth.
What a bitter taste.

Excuses
(2024)

Justice will be elusive,

No idea, 'til when.

As long as we're served excuses,

half-truths, or even fabricated ones;

As long as we're dazzled by the
'reality shows' in the house,
senate, and the palace;

As long as reasons such as,
"Your Honor, hindi ko na po maalala," or

"I invoke my right against self-incrimination"

are welcomed with eyes closed and a sigh;

As long as we clutch our stomachs,
guffawing at the memes of this nauseating reasoning

and let them rub our bellies to sleep
when we should've kept our eyes open;

Justice will keep slipping away from our grasp,

and our brighter tomorrow will remain a dream
until the day we die.

Lapdogs
(2024)

Because we love to stop,
Smell the roses,
and stay fallen into a deep slumber
in the meadow of our illusions,
we continue to be lapdogs
whose purpose is just to follow
and sniff our so-called 'masters'
from behind,
the stench of their debris
are scent to our clouded nostrils;
and we remain content
with the morsel
when we should have relished
in the manna of the land
that we must call our own.

About the Author

Aliena

Aliena was the name behind the supplement "Baboy Ko (at Iba Pang Taludturang Kuwento)," published by Ukiyoto in 2022, and the novel "I'm Here," published in the early months of 2024. She discovered her love for writing when she was still in elementary school. In fact, her hobby of reading available textbooks in her school encouraged her to create a mock textbook of her own. Little did she know that from that simple dream, she would have the chance to turn it into reality. During her later years in grade school, she came across a literary folio tackling various taboo issues, which inspired her to write her own poems using old notebooks. In high school, she started creating funny comic books based on her favorite TV shows, particularly World Wrestling Entertainment (her high level of motivation caused her to use about three big notebooks at that time).

It was also in high school when she made a name for herself with her skills in essay writing and song competitions, earning her gold medals in school-level contests (national for songs). Unfortunately, even though she came to love journalism at that age, she never received recognition for her extracurricular activities. She attributed it to the fact that she only wrote for the sake of having her name published. Despite receiving some major awards related to writing, the author strongly dislikes contests,

competing, and coaching alike.

As a poet, Aliena loves to use strong vocabulary and does not shy away from the literal and figurative filth, as she believes these words send a strong message to the audience.

Aliena pursued a Bachelor of Secondary Education, majoring in English, at Central Luzon State University in Nueva Ecija, Philippines, as it offered two subjects that were close to her heart: Campus Journalism and Creative Writing. However, she soon realized that true learning comes from continuous exploration and practice.

The author has served as an English teacher for more than 10 years. Some of her tasks include teaching creative writing and, for the longest time, school paper management, where she witnessed the journey of the writers from the bitterness of defeat to the sweetness of victory. It was also in that profession where she met her better half, "Manong," and had two adorable and talented kids.

Currently, Aliena continues to work on her other books, with no more aspirations than to continue the dream that she once had at a young age.

www.ingramcontent.com/pod-product-compliance
Lightning Source LLC
LaVergne TN
LVHW041635070526
838199LV00052B/3376